So You Want to Be...

NICK

UNfabulous!™

By Addie Singer (and friends!)

12 11 10 9 8 7 6 5 4 3 2 1   6 7 8 9 10/0

Printed in Mexico   First printing, May 2006

Note: The information from these websites was considered valid as of the date of publication of this book. Scholastic does not monitor these websites on an ongoing basis and it is important to remember that their content and ownership can change over time. Parents/teachers should check these sites prior to future access by children.

SCHOLASTIC INC.

New York   Toronto   London   Auckland   Sydney
Mexico City   New Delhi   Hong Kong   Buenos Aires

Did you ever have one of those days? You know, the kind when nothing seems to go quite right? You leave your math homework at home; you forgot to study for your history test. You drop your lunch in the cafeteria, and then fall into it — face-first. And just when you think it's finally over, your loving big brother forgets to pick you up after school, and you end up waiting for hours. Outside. In the rain.

Welcome to my life.

But see, that's not the whole story. Because when things go wrong, there are plenty of people to help make them right again. My awesome best friends, Zach and Geena. My dog, Nancy. My parents. And even my brother, Ben . . . sometimes. No matter how many times I trip and fall on my face, there's always someone there to help me up again. Even the biggest disasters have happy endings!

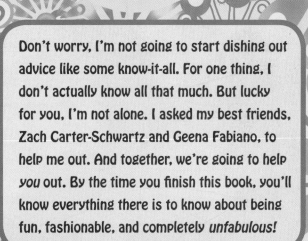

Yes, my life is messy. But you know what? That's what makes things interesting. So if you're looking for advice on how to make your life nice, neat, and perfect, you've got the wrong book! I can't tell you much about how to be perfect — ask anyone. But I *can* tell you what it's like to be me. I can tell you how to have fun with your friends and what to do when they're not around, how to save your personal style and how to save the world. And I can tell you how awesome life can be . . . even when it's a little less than perfect.

Don't worry, I'm not going to start dishing out advice like some know-it-all. For one thing, I don't actually know all that much. But lucky for you, I'm not alone. I asked my best friends, Zach Carter-Schwartz and Geena Fabiano, to help me out. And together, we're going to help *you* out. By the time you finish this book, you'll know everything there is to know about being fun, fashionable, and completely *unfabulous!*

Thank you, thank you. All this applause just for me? I guess you like me, you really like me! I'd like to thank —

Oops, sorry. I get a little carried away sometimes, dreaming of the day when I'm a world-famous superstar. See, I play the guitar, and I write all my own songs. So I figure, someday, I could be a star.

Hey, it could happen!

But you know what? I don't need fame and fortune. Not yet, anyway. Because I just love the way singing and playing make me feel. It's like, when I've got that guitar in my hands, all my troubles just drift away. I think it's because I can say whatever I need to say. If you ask me, music isn't about talent, it isn't about knowing the notes — it's all about expressing yourself.

And what could be better than that?

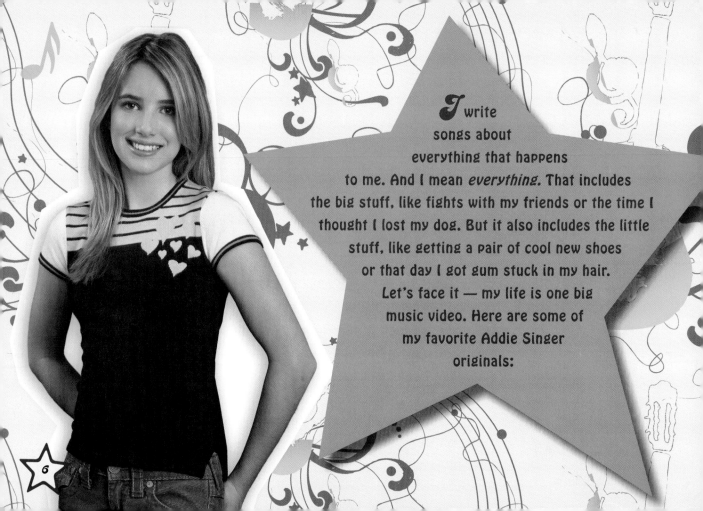

I write songs about everything that happens to me. And I mean *everything.* That includes the big stuff, like fights with my friends or the time I thought I lost my dog. But it also includes the little stuff, like getting a pair of cool new shoes or that day I got gum stuck in my hair. Let's face it — my life is one big music video. Here are some of my favorite Addie Singer originals:

I can't drive, and I can't vote,
I can't even pierce my nose,
So what does it mean . . . to
    be thirteen?
I can go to the movies and
    see . . . PG-Thirteen!
(Can't see it when you're twelve!)
PG-Thirteen!
PG-Thirteen!
PG-Thirteen!

Laundry dog, laundry dog,
Don't let the "Tide" take her away.
HOWWWWWWL.

New shoes, you rule!
You rule, new shoes!
New shoes, you rule!
You rule, new shoes!

Tossed my cookies on a yellow bus,
Bus Driver Bob, he sure did cuss.
At least I got to stay home,
That's the upside of food poisoning.

So what do *you* have to say for yourself?
Use this space to write your own song lyrics.

_____

_____

_____

_____

_____

_____

_____

_____

When I joined this band called CUTE, I thought I had it made. Turns out, not so much. Because CUTE didn't play their instruments. They didn't sing. All they did was . . . *dance*. And since I can barely walk down the hall without falling down, I figured dancing was *definitely* off-limits. But I got a big surprise: Dancing is easy. No, really. The key is to stop worrying about being a great dancer, and just focus on having fun. Here's how I did it:

* If you don't know what to do with your arms and legs, just copy everyone else.
* Practice at home in your room where no one can see you.
* Pretend you know what you're doing. (I promise, no one will figure out the truth.)
* Close your eyes, so you can pretend no one's watching.
* Keep in mind, no one actually knows how to dance. They're all just as clueless as you!

The most awesome, unfabulous dance songs are:

_____

_____

_____

_____

Anything by Addie Singer!

Relationships 101

It seems like, when it comes to relationships, everybody's got an opinion. And even though people constantly want to put their two cents in, it's most important to listen to yourself. I mean, I know my aunt Bertha was just trying to help when she tried to talk to me about dating, but it's not exactly the number one topic I'd want to discuss with a lady whose main pastimes included flossing, scarfing down Italian pastries, and knitting lumpy sweaters with animals on them. Here's the song I wrote about Aunt Bertha's attempts to dish out love advice:

Aunt Bertha, Aunt Bertha, there's no one better
If you like buckteeth and rhinoceros sweaters.
I know she means well but as far as I can tell
She knows nothing of kissing with braces.
(And if she did, I wouldn't want to know.)

Though it was sweet of Aunt Bertha to try, her advice wasn't exactly what I was looking for. Here's some relationship advice I actually could have used when I was seriously crushing on

Randy Klein:

- If you see the person you like in the halls,

    DO say hello to him.

    DON'T scream and run the other way.

- When you are selecting an outfit to impress the person you have a crush on,

    DO pick out something that flatters you and makes you feel comfortable.

    DON'T forget to wear pants.

- If you get nervous when you see your crush around,

    DO try to imagine having a pleasant conversation with him.

    DON'T imagine yourself being whisked away by helicopters.

- When trying to make your crush laugh,

    DO show him your funniest impression of your dog.

    DON'T show him your funniest impression of his mom.

- If you want to invite your crush out to do something fun,

    DO ask him to meet you at a basketball game or other sporting event.

    DON'T invite him to come with you for your yearly checkup.

- When coming up with an icebreaker to use on your crush,

    DO tell him he reminds you of one of your best friends.

    DON'T tell him he reminds you of Bigfoot.

These are just some of the basics. Hope they help! And, like Aunt Bertha, I'm no expert on these things. So, as with any advice — it's totally up to you. You can either take it or leave it!

13

I used to worry about being invisible. Sometimes it just felt like people were looking right through me. One day I decided that there was only one way to fix that: I needed to get famous. Fast. So I joined the band called CUTE — I was going to be a star! Just one problem: CUTE was *so* not me. I mean, you won't believe the song they wanted me to sing:

I'm such a cute girl.
Living in a cute world.
Cute, cute, cute, cute, cute, cute, cute.
Look at my cute toes.
Look at my cute clothes.
Cute shoes, cute hair, cute, cute, cute.
You will never be . . .
Half as cute as me . . .
We're such cute girls.
Living in a cute world.
Cute, cute, cute, cute, cute!

And I almost went through with it. After all, I figured, what's more important than being famous? Then, at the last minute, I figured it out. There is something more important than being famous: *being yourself*. So when I finally got on stage, here's what I sang instead:

Maybe I'll be famous someday, maybe I won't. But one thing's for sure: I'm always going to be myself, no matter what.

I can't be a fake girl living in a fake world.
Fake, fake, fake, fake, fake, fake, fake.
I write my own songs.
Even if they're all wrong.
Hey, sometimes they're sorta good.
You may not agree.
But at least they're me.
I am a real girl living in a real world.
Real, real, real, real, real, real, real.

Everyone wants to be a star!
What will you be famous for?

Fabiano's Unfabulous Fashion

By Geena Fabiano

She's original!
She's sociable!
She's fashionable!

She's . . . GEENA FABIANO!

16

Listen to Addie; she knows what she's talking about. At least, the part where she told you to listen to me. I know I'm not a famous fashion designer yet, but trust me, I will be. I like to think of my personal style as a mirror of my inner self. So, you know, it totally rocks. And someday, everyone who's anyone will be wearing a Geena Fabiano original.

That's right, I said original. As in, I make my own style. See, lots of people think that the key to being fashionable is looking like everyone else. No way! I'll let you in on the real secret: Being stylish is about being yourself. I make my own clothes and accessories so that the whole world can see who Geena Fabiano really is.

Here's how I do it!

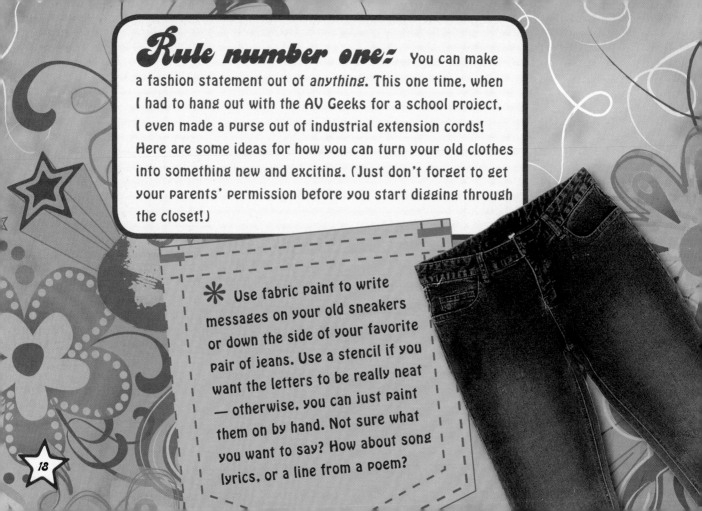

Rule number one: You can make a fashion statement out of *anything*. This one time, when I had to hang out with the AV Geeks for a school project, I even made a purse out of industrial extension cords! Here are some ideas for how you can turn your old clothes into something new and exciting. (Just don't forget to get your parents' permission before you start digging through the closet!)

✳ Use fabric paint to write messages on your old sneakers or down the side of your favorite pair of jeans. Use a stencil if you want the letters to be really neat — otherwise, you can just paint them on by hand. Not sure what you want to say? How about song lyrics, or a line from a poem?

✳ Brighten up an old tank top with a colorful trim. Punch little holes in a line all around the bottom of the tank top. Leave about half an inch between each hole. Now find a pretty colored string or ribbon, and lace it through the holes, just like you would lace up your sneaker. Tie the ends in a bow.

✳ Use a bleach pen to personalize your old T-shirts, sneakers, skirts, socks, anything! Just apply the bleach, leave it on for about ten minutes, then wipe it off with an old towel. When you rinse and dry the item, you'll see that the color has faded everywhere you put the bleach.

✳ Turn an ordinary shirt into an adorable off-the-shoulder tee. Cut off the collar of the shirt (cut around an imaginary line about a half inch from the top). Now cut off the edges of each sleeve (a half inch from the edge of the sleeve). On each sleeve, loop a ribbon into the sleeve and out through the collar. Next pull it tight and tie it in a bow. Now you're ready for the runway!

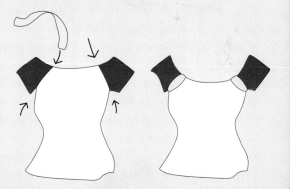

Before I
get started
on a new design, I like to do
some brainstorming. You know,
come up with the wildest,
craziest outfit ideas that I can.
I draw pictures of them, just
like a real fashion designer,
and decide which ones I like.
And then I figure out how
to make my crazy fashion
dreams come true.

What would your dream outfit look like?
Use this space to brainstorm!

Now that you've got your fantastic new outfit, it's time to accessorize. But why waste your allowance on accessories when you can just make them yourself?

✳ Find a pretty piece of fabric, like a long velvet ribbon or a sequined cord. You can cut it to whatever length you want and use it as a belt, a hair ribbon, a choker, or a scarf.

✳ Flip-flops are the hottest way to keep your feet cool. Use household glue to decorate yours with cloth flowers, beads, and sequins.

✳ Wanna go retro? Cut the sleeves off of an old sweatshirt and turn them into leg warmers. For decoration, you can sew a strip of colorful cloth around the top, or as a stripe down the side.

My latest creation:
Geena's Wraparound Ribbon Belt

1. Cut a piece of ribbon long enough to wrap around your waist with about eight inches hanging down.

2. Cut fourteen more pieces of ribbon all the same length. Use a bunch of different colors.

3. Take three pieces of ribbon and braid them together. Leave four inches unbraided at each end.

4. Keep making braids until you run out of ribbons. You should have five braids total.

5. Tie the braids together, end to end, until you have one really, really long braid.

6. Now wrap it around your waist as many times as you can. Tie it into a knot or a bow on the side, leaving some ribbon hanging down, and you've got yourself a funky, chunky ribbon belt.

Fashion Police

Ever wish you could get a glimpse of your permanent record? Well, I finally did — and it wasn't pretty. You won't believe what the school counselor wrote about me:

Ms. Fabiano's tendency toward inappropriate dress stems from a deep-seated insecurity. Her flashy outfits are a cry for attention.

I mean, seriously — could she be any more wrong? At first I was a little worried. *Was* I insecure? *Were* my outfits inappropriate? I gave it a lot of thought. And you know what I decided? No.

No way. Nohow. No, no, no, no. Never.

The counselor just didn't get me. My outfits aren't about getting attention — they're about being myself. Can I help it if "myself" is totally fashion-forward? Well, I couldn't let my permanent record be that wrong. So . . . I made a few changes:

Ms. Fabiano's bold outfits reflect her creativity and unique style. Only a student with a strong sense of self-worth and no insecurities would be brave enough to wear clothes of her own design.
P.S. Please excuse Geena from all future detentions.

Now *that's* more like it!

Zach Saves the World
(And So Can You!)
By Zach Carter-Schwartz

He's a science whiz.
He's a basketball star.
He loves the environment!

He's . . . ZACH CARTER-SCHWARTZ

Did you know that recycling one soda can saves enough energy to run your television for three hours? Or that there are thousands of animal species in danger of going extinct? How about that one dripping sink wastes more than *500* gallons of water a year?

I think of the environment as like a basketball game. You know, there are all these different players doing all these different jobs. And making one little mistake can affect the whole game. You miss the ball. The other team steals it. They shoot. They score. And that's it — game over. Uh . . . not that something like that has ever happened to me. But trust me: Little changes can add up to *big* results.

That can be scary, but it can also be great. Because it means that everyone can do something to change the world. Every small thing you do — recycling a soda can or picking up a piece of litter or marching in a rally for insect rights — can have a big effect. I try to change the world a little bit each day. Now you can, too!

My biggest cause is the environment. I even made a movie about it last year: *Lo, the Pollution Monster Cometh!* It was awesome. I made little clay people and used stop-motion photography. Addie's dog played the pollution monster. This year I'm working on *Lo, the Oil Spill Cometh!* I'm just having a little trouble getting the fake baby seals to look exactly right. Hmm . . . do you think that if I roll them under the soda machine, the dust balls will look like fur?

What causes do you believe in?

_____

_____

_____

_____

_____

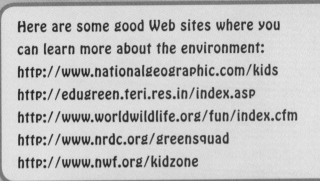

Here are some good Web sites where you can learn more about the environment:

http://www.nationalgeographic.com/kids
http://edugreen.teri.res.in/index.asp
http://www.worldwildlife.org/fun/index.cfm
http://www.nrdc.org/greensquad
http://www.nwf.org/kidzone

Once you decide what's wrong in the world, you can start figuring out how to fix it!

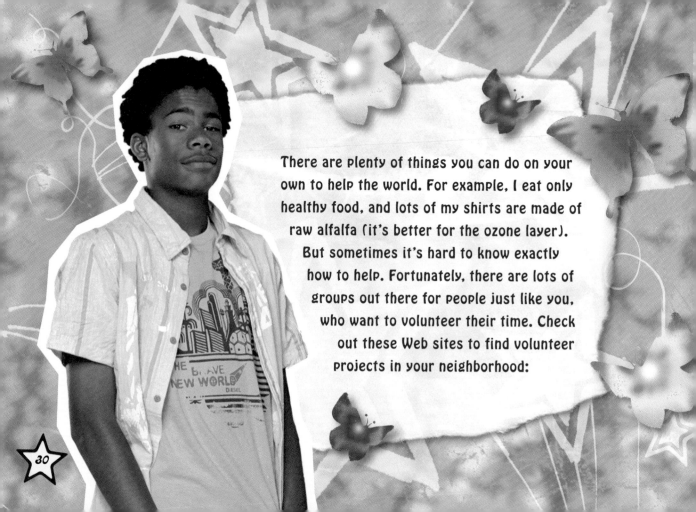

There are plenty of things you can do on your own to help the world. For example, I eat only healthy food, and lots of my shirts are made of raw alfalfa (it's better for the ozone layer). But sometimes it's hard to know exactly how to help. Fortunately, there are lots of groups out there for people just like you, who want to volunteer their time. Check out these Web sites to find volunteer projects in your neighborhood:

http://www.idealist.org/kt/volunteercenter.html
Everything you could ever want to know about volunteering, including what it is and how you can do it. The site has links to organizations all over the country, and advice on how you can get started.

http://www.kidscare.org
There are Kids Care clubs all over the country. They do monthly projects to improve their communities. The site has instructions for how you and your friends can start your own club.

http://www.geocities.com/HelpfulHandsjr/
Created and run by kids, Helpful Hands collects food for the needy, throws parties for the elderly, and makes Thanksgiving dinners for foster children. The site even has suggestions for how you can start your own volunteer projects.

http://www.dosomething.org/
This group's slogan is "Young people changing their world," and Do Something has suggestions for what you can do to help. If you come up with an idea for a project of your own, Do Something can help you figure out how to pay for it.

http://www.volunteermatch.org/
A nationwide database that will match you up with volunteer programs in your own neighborhood, wherever you live.

Of course, you don't have to join someone else's project. You can start one of your own. Like that time I held a one-man sit-in to save the tree frogs. Here are some other things you and your friends can do:

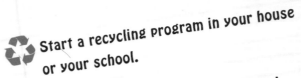 Start a recycling program in your house or your school.

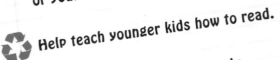 Help teach younger kids how to read.

Hold a food drive for the needy.

Collect toys, games, or clothes to donate to people who can't afford them.

Visit a retirement home and make friends with the residents.

Spend a day cleaning up litter.

Three things you can do this year to help the world:

_____

_____

_____

With Friends Like These . . .

By Addie Singer
(with a little help from her friends!)

It's me, Addie, back again because it's time to take care of the most important element in your fabulous life: your friends. Zach, Geena, and I have been friends ever since I can remember. I know some people only want to be friends with people who are just like them — but that's definitely not us. We're totally different from one another. And that's exactly what makes us work.

We do everything for one another. And I mean *everything*. Geena and I help Zach out with all of his weird save-the-world causes. Zach and I let Geena use us as guinea pigs for her latest fashion innovations. And, of course, Zach and Geena listen to all my new songs. . . . And they also listen to me talk about Randy Klein 24/7.

Sure, we get into fights sometimes. Sometimes we even get into *food* fights. . . . Fortunately, Boston cream pie comes out in the wash. But we never forget what's really important: one another!

The Perfect Present

My dad has got to be the worst present-giver of all time. This year, he really hit the jackpot. He gave my mom a kissing-fish cookie jar. Of course, it's not all his fault. It's tough to pick out presents for people, even people you know really well. That's why Geena, Zach, and I like to make one another presents. That way you can come up with something that's really perfect — and totally unique.

Make-Your-Own Present Ideas:

✿ Burn a CD of all your friend's favorite songs — or songs that make you think of her.

✿ Write your own song. Like, last year I wrote my mom a birthday song. It went like this:

> She can stand on her head, she can cook for ten!
> If she hadn't been born, there'd be no me or Ben!
> She's Mom. She's Mom. She's the bomb.
> Yeah—she's Mom.

✿ Decorate a picture frame, then put a photo of you and your friends inside.

✿ Send a donation to a charity in your friend's name. This is Zach's suggestion. Last year, he gave a donation to the Endangered Bumblebee Society for my birthday.

Every great friendship needs a great hangout, and for us, it's *Juice!* That's this great juice bar where they serve the best smoothies you've ever tasted. Zach, Geena, and I go there almost every day — and almost everything exciting that's ever happened to us has happened at *Juice!*

Top 5 Juice! moments:

5. Singing onstage with the band CUTE – my first real gig!
4. Turning on the blender without a lid, so the smoothie blew up in Ben's face. Okay, that was just my fantasy, but in my imagination it was awesome!
3. Hiding out on class picture day . . . only to find out that the whole school had the same idea!
2. Sharing smoothies with Zach and Geena that time we made up after a fight. Uh . . . okay, after *all* our fights.
1. Getting recognized by a fan after I published my first article in the school newspaper.

Of course, the best thing about *Juice!* is its delicious smoothies. They have so many flavors — Orange-tastic, Razmatazz, Mocha Moo-Cow — the list goes on forever. The problem is, my allowance doesn't. So sometimes, Geena, Zach, and I stay home and make smoothies for ourselves. My brother, Ben, works at *Juice!*, and he snagged us some of their best recipes:

Precious Peach

2 cups peach nectar (juice)
1 cup vanilla frozen yogurt
1 cup peach yogurt
$\frac{1}{2}$ banana
$1\frac{1}{2}$ cups frozen peach slices

Put all the ingredients into the blender and blend until smooth.

Strawberry Surprise

6 ice cubes
16 strawberries
$\frac{1}{2}$ cup frozen concentrated limeade
$\frac{1}{2}$ cup water

Put the ice cubes into the blender first, and blend until they're crushed. Then add the rest of the ingredients and blend until smooth.

Banana-rama

$\frac{1}{2}$ cup fresh orange juice
$\frac{1}{2}$ cup nonfat yogurt
$\frac{1}{4}$ cup blueberries, washed
1 frozen banana

Put ingredients in a blender and . . . well, you know what to do next!

39

*W*hen I played sick to skip out on the Tristate Sporting Goods Trade Show, I thought I had it made. My dad wanted to make a whole big trip out of it — he thought the trade show would be the most exciting event of the year. Uh, hello? Football-helmet demonstrations and lectures about the latest trends in athletic socks? Not my idea of a good time. So I gave the parents my best "I'm too sick to get out of bed" act, and they bought it. They went off to the trade show and I got to stay home alone . . . well, home with Ben. Almost the same thing. So I was home free, right?

Wrong. Mom called me *every hour on the hour* to see how I was feeling. It meant I couldn't leave the house! It meant Zach, Geena, and I couldn't go to *Juice!* — we couldn't even finish a game of Monopoly! I was seriously bored. Bored out of my mind. Like, so bored I would rather have been at the trade show. Okay, well, I wasn't *that* bored!

I vowed I would never let myself get that bored again, which is why I put together this list. Here, from me to you, is the first ever . . .

LIST OF STUFF TO DO WHEN YOU'RE TRAPPED BY THE PHONE BECAUSE YOUR MOM'S CALLING YOU EVERY HOUR ON THE HOUR

- Create your own board game. Use a big, flat piece of cardboard or construction paper as the game board. If your game has place names, use places you know and love, or places you've always wanted to go. Make up a set of rules and create your own rule book.
- Have a during-the-day sleepover party, complete with popcorn, sleeping bags, and scary stories.
- Write an episode of your favorite TV show. Assign a part to each of your friends. If you have a video camera, you can even tape it, and then watch yourself on TV!
- Geena says nothing beats makeover madness: Get all your makeup together and try it on in wild combinations! Give yourself a supermodel hairdo, and you're ready for the runway. Or at least, you're ready to parade back and forth across your bedroom.

And when you've only got five minutes left before the call and you and your friends need a quick way to have fun . . .

- Simon Says
- Funny face contest
- Staring contest
- Hangman
- 20 Questions
- Charades

41

Extra! Extra! Extracurricular!

Just because I already have two really great friends doesn't mean I don't want any more. And joining after-school clubs and extracurricular activities can be a great way to make new friends. For example, when I joined the school newspaper, I got to know Mary Ferry. At first she pretty much hated me because I didn't proofread my article for the "My Turn" feature. (How did I miss the giant headline reading MY TURD? I'll never live it down!) But now we're totally friends.

My brother, Ben, was in so many clubs that he's on every single page of his middle-school yearbook. So you can thank him for this list of ideas. But you shouldn't actually thank him . . . because then he'll find out that I snuck his yearbook out of his room.

Student council
Cooking club
Community service club
Auto shop club
Debate team
Mathletes
Newspaper *This is the one activity Ben didn't do, which is why I went for it. Trust me, it's fun. Just don't forget to proofread!*

If your school doesn't have anything you like, why not start your own club?
If you could do any after-school activities you wanted, what would they be?

_____

_____

_____

Okay, so now that you've got all these friends, why not get them all together in one place and P-A-R-T-Y! I'll admit it: I used to kind of hate parties. Mainly because I'm such a klutz. Randy Klein has these big annual back-to-school parties, and every year, I fall into something and make a huge fool out of myself. In front of the *entire* class. A couple years ago, I fell into a pile of mud and everyone called me Mudzilla for months! This year, I had a party of my own, and I vowed nothing embarrassing would happen. Well, guess what? It did. I fell *splat* onto a plate of nachos and landed with my head in the punch bowl. And guess what else? I didn't even care. It was *still* the best party ever — and I can't wait to throw another one!

Party-Planning Basics

Step 1 is tough, but unavoidable: You gotta get your parents' permission. I tried my best to figure out a way around that one. Trust me, it doesn't work. So just cross your fingers and ask for their permission . . . and then ask them to stay upstairs and out of the way.

Once you get Step 1 out of the way, it's time for the real party-planning fun to begin. Step 2 is figuring out these important basics:

Location   Music   Food   Guest list   Theme

Lights, Camera, P-A-R-T-Y!

The next party Zach, Geena, and I throw is going to be a movie-themed party. Here's what we're going to need:

* Red carpet running down the front entryway (Try using a long piece of red felt.)
* Lots of flashing lights when people walk in, to look like paparazzi
* An invitation made up to look like a movie ticket
* Movie posters quoting fake critics' reviews ("This is the best party of the year!" "I laughed, I cried, I danced until my feet went numb!")
* And, of course, lots and *lots* of popcorn

I know I sound like I've got it all figured out, but trust me, I'm just making it up as I go along. I mean, it's easy enough to say "Just be yourself" — it's another thing to do it. Once, I got so worried that the real me wasn't good enough that I made myself into a completely different person. I read this article in *Glossy Teen* magazine that told me I should wear high heels and giggle a lot, so that's exactly what I did. And you know what? It blew up in my face. I thought acting like someone else would make people like me better. Turns out it just made people think I was a little delusional.

So I decided: Never again would I try to be someone I'm not. Sure, there are things I'd like to change about myself. For one thing, I'm a huge klutz. And sometimes I worry that my hair is kind of flat. But that stuff doesn't really matter, right? It's just part of who I am. So I try to focus on the other stuff — all the things I *do* love about myself. Here's my list:

Top 5 Things to Love About Addie Singer
(That's Me!)

5. I play the guitar and write all my own songs.

4. I have awesome friends.

3. I look super cute in that hot-pink shirt with the tiny blue flowers on it.

2. I'm good at making people laugh. (I'm a natural at it!)

1. I am totally, completely, absolutely *unfabulous* — and that's okay!

Okay, your turn. Time to stop obsessing about what's wrong with you and start being proud of what's right. What makes you awesome and unfabulous? What makes your friends want to hang out with you? What would you never, ever want to change about yourself?

Top Five Things to Love About You

5. _____

4. _____

3. _____

2. _____

1. _____

Like I said before, life can get messy. But now you've officially got all you need to dig through the mess and find the good stuff. Just make sure you have plenty of unfabulous fun along the way!